Wanda
and the  Alien to the
the
Rescue

Sue Hendra

For our Wanda with love from Mummy and Daddy

WANDA AND THE ALIEN TO THE RESCUE
A RED FOX BOOK 978 1 849 41587 3
Published in Great Britain by Red Fox,
an imprint of Random House Children's Publishers UK
A Random House Group Company
This edition published 2013
1 3 5 7 9 10 8 6 4 2
Copyright © Paul Linnet and Sue Hendra, 2013
Red Fox Books are published by Random House Children's Publishers UK,
61– 63 Uxbridge Road, London, W5 5SA
www.randomhouse.co.uk   www.randomhousechildrens.co.uk
Addresses for companies within The Random House Group Limited can be found at:
www.randomhouse.co.uk/offices.htm
THE RANDOM HOUSE GROUP Limited Reg. No. 954009
A CIP catalogue record for this book is available from the British Library
Printed in China

The Random House Group Limited supports the Forest Stewardship Council® (FSC®), the leading
international forest-certification organisation. Our books carrying the FSC label are printed on FSC®-certified paper.
FSC is the only forest-certification scheme supported by the leading environmental organisations, including Greenpeace.
Our paper procurement policy can be found at www.randomhouse.co.uk/environment

Wanda and the alien were splashing in puddles,
when they heard a strange noise . . . *Squeak, squeak!*
"Did you hear that?" said Wanda.

"Hmm," thought the alien. "Maybe it's a spaceship?

Or a robot . . . that's malfunctioned."

"Maybe it's an oober joober bird?" thought Wanda.

They followed the sound and it led them to a bush.
"LOOK!" cried Wanda . . .

There in the leaves, looking cold,
wet and frightened, was a little creature!

Wanda held the creature
and stroked him while
the alien looked
for his mummy.

He left no stone unturned,

searched high and low.

He even went back to the spaceship to get his special binoculars.

But the little creature's mummy was nowhere in sight.

By now it was starting
to get dark.
"We can't leave him out here
on his own," said Wanda.
"Let's take him home and decide
what to do in the morning."
"SQUEAK!" squeaked
the little creature.

Back at Wanda's house it was bath time. The alien prepared some custard to wash the creature in . . . "No," said Wanda, "that's not quite right!"

They washed him with soapy water instead
and dried him with a hairdryer.

"He must be hungry," said Wanda.
"But what does he eat?"
They both made their favourite
dishes to try and tempt him.
But the creature had other ideas.

After supper, it was time for bed,
but where was the creature going to sleep?
Wanda got out her tools, the alien drew a plan,
and they set to work to make a little bed.

However, the
creature didn't
seem very tired . . .

. . . in fact, he was full of beans!

"Maybe we could sing him to sleep?"
thought Wanda.

Wanda went to get her guitar
to play him a gentle lullaby.
But the alien had a lullaby of his own.

"Wait," said Wanda.
"I think perhaps a quieter
song might be better."

At long last, after much changing of beds, they all settled down to sleep.

First thing in the morning they sat down to breakfast. The creature wanted custard again. "Custard for breakfast?" thought Wanda.

They had to admit though, it was good. Especially with a few added ingredients.

With their tummies full,
they got ready to go and
find the creature's mummy.
Wanda went to fetch her
trolley so the creature
could have a ride . . .

But when she got back,
he was nowhere to be found!

They looked high and low.

They looked far and wide.

They left no stone unturned.

Then they heard the sound of an engine . . .

"There he is!" Wanda cried. "He's in your space rocket, and he's started the engine!"

Luckily, the alien knew just what to do.

"You're a little rascal, aren't you?"
said Wanda to the creature.

Just then they heard a very big
***SQUEAK!* and it was coming**
towards them.

It was the little creature's mummy.
She had found them!
"Thank you for taking such good
care of my little one," she said.
"That's all right," said Wanda.
"It was fun."

The two friends waved a fond goodbye,
and headed back to Wanda's house.

**It was very peaceful with just the two of them again.
It had been quite an adventure, but it was time to**

put their feet up, and have a well-deserved rest.
Suddenly, there was a knock at the door . . .

Wanda and the alien had done such a good job
looking after the little creature

**that his mummy thought the whole family
should come and visit.**

It looked as though Wanda and the alien would
have to stock up on custard — they would be
getting lots of visits from their new friends.

And so, with their tummies full,
they settled down for a nice story.